T.B.O.R.

The Book Of Richard

Based on a true story...

Richard W. Aites

AmErica House
Baltimore

Copyright 2000 by Richard W. Aites.
All rights reserved. No part of this book may be reproduced in any form without written permission from the publishers, except by a reviewer who may quote brief passages in a review to be printed in a newspaper or magazine.

First printing

ISBN: 1-58851-001-8
PUBLISHED BY AMERICA HOUSE BOOK PUBLISHERS
www.publishamerica.com
Baltimore

Printed in the United States of America

This book is dedicated to the wonderful Doctors and Nurses of the Cardinal Glennon N.I.C.U. of the greater St. Louis. Without your knowledge and caring this story could not have been written.
Thanks again for saving my son's life.

And to the memory of my grandmother:
Mattie Ossenfort, who was, is and will always be the little part of goodness one never loses.

And finally, my colleagues Scot Haywood and Denise Bosse, who brought me out of the stone age by opening up windows.

And to my Aunt Dovie who always had faith in me. And my parents who always prevailed through the most trying of times.

*Inka.
Truly an inspiration.
Thanks for always being there.
Richard W ___*

OPENING

I have read the writings of many scholars of my time whom take away from your words, your actions, even that of your miracles. It appears as though their gained wisdom which brings them wealth here, is the destroyer of their faith.

Know ye Lord, that your divine inspiration and beauty is instilled upon the hearts of a great multitude.

Without you, we are nothing...

THE BOOK OF RICHARD

FOREWORD

As I focused into the quiet corridor while awaiting to present my testimony to the grand jury, I reviewed the case in mind. I visualized arriving on the scene with victim screaming hysterically and covered in blood. I saw my patrol supervisor rendering first aid to the victim's severed hand while I proceeded to kick in the deadbolted apartment door in an attempt to apprehend the suspect.

As I entered the darkened living quarters, I observed a large amount of blood covering the living room floor. I found the suspect, high on crack cocaine, standing in the rear bedroom. A crazed look was in his eyes as he clutched the large knife behind his back. "The voices told me to kill her," he would later state after being taken into custody. Then my mind wandered to another recent incident, when I had to confront a suicidal subject intoxicated on rum and armed with a fully loaded 9mm pistol and .22 caliber rifle. The big, burly suspect was irate with the notion of killing his neighbors and any police officer that just happened to get in the way.

Several officers tried to negotiate with the suspect, however all attempts failed. To gain the suspect's trust, I had to holster my service pistol and face him one-on-one while his weapons remained at his side. Fortunately as I stood but ten meters from his position, I was able to develop a rapport with the heavily armed man and draw him away from his weapons. He was taken into custody, unharmed. I thought about the violence I had witnessed over the previous year and of the recent rash of school shootings. I reflected upon the miracle of my infant son, his birth, his near death and the miraculous recovery. I contemplated his future and the thought of him witnessing or experiencing such violence brought a cold shudder to my mid section.

From under the subpoena and two copies of the police report that were resting upon my lap, I removed a letter which I had intended on reviewing while awaiting the hearing. The letter would be the opening 'synopsis' of a 100 page manuscript titled 'T.B.O.R.' short for 'The Book of Richard'.

The opening paragraph read: *To my beloved son: Chayce Richard, who is also known as Emmanuel. I write this in the hope that someday you will understand it's meaning. This letter is but a summary as to what follows in the form of testimonials and devotionals. The sole purpose of this book is to make you aware of the blessing bestowed upon you by our Lord Jesus Christ. For as long as you walk on this earth, you shall recognize his presence.*

I then reviewed the second paragraph which tells of the violence of this culture and the identity crisis within it, a generation without God. I did make it known that there is still much good in the world and that it is the goodness in people that he should emulate. I further gave him this advice: *Believe in yourself and be of yourself. Do not let society or any one person dictate who you are. Do not envy those who are stronger or wiser but find friendship in the nature of their being, for then you shall possess a greater strength and wisdom which is not of the world. Do not succumb to those who lead you down the paths of destruction through drugs or violence, but be patient with them and teach them what they did not know. Rebellion is human nature, yet spend more time learning than rebelling. Give to those in need and feed them hungry, but do not steal for them, for you are blessed and shall possess many gifts.*

Stand strong against you adversary but before conflict, make amends. Be strong yet be kind, that your friends be many and enemies, few. Again my son, stay away from drugs and alcohol for the se substances shall hold you back by cluttering your mind and weakening your spirits.

As I flipped the page over, the opening of a door and the muffled voices of many people caught my attention. The Prosecuting Attorney hen stepped out from behind the door.

"Officer, we're ready for your testimony."

Ten minutes later I left the courtroom. When I stepped into the court clerk's office to sign out, the buzzer went off above my head.

"Congratulations," the attractive, middle-aged woman said. "That's a true bill. Your case is going to trial."

As I left the justice center, a silent thought came across my mind. The thought became a prayer. I prayed that if I were to fall in the line of duty before my son had reached the age of understanding, I prayed that the testimony in 'T.B.O.R' would help him realize that violence is an adversary and not something to be envied as it is by the generation before his.

This will be the most important testimony of my life as my young son will be its benefactor, its jury…

THE BOOK OF RICHARD

PRELUDE

On a frigid night in late winter of 1984, a young boy made his way across the small, northwestern Pennsylvania town and into a snow covered forest. Guided by the light of a full moon, his journey led him to a frozen river where kneeled a long the stream's edge. He then focused into the clear night sky, onto the constellation 'ORION'. The boy recited the 'Lord's Prayer' and announced to the heavens that he had brought himself to believe that Jesus Christ was truly the son of God.

Several moments later an undescribable feeling came over the boy. He was overwhelmed with fear as he realized that he was not alone in the frozen forest. The hair on the back of his neck stood straight up as his sixth sense recognized the presence behind him. "Amen," he finished as he stood to his feet and turned to face the visitor.

Standing next to a lifeless tree, some fifty meters down the river's bank, stood a form immersed in a brilliant, white light. The figure was that of a man draped in a long, white robe. The boy suddenly overcame his fear and slowly approached the man. As the lad closed to within thirty meters, the figure faded into the light and a moment later, the light faded into darkness.

The boy returned home later that evening and wrote the event down in a scroll. He wanted desperately to share his experience however being surrounded by non-believers, he was afraid that his sanity would be questioned. Therefore he placed the scroll in a glass jar and hid it up on the mountain at a place called 'Big Rocks'.

THE BOOK OF RICHARD

CHAPTER ONE

The heavy pounding of the propellers from the arm-laden gunships created a whirlwind of waves upon the ocean's surface. Two minutes later, four twin prop CH-46 helicopters travelling in a diamond formation, thundered overhead. Their destination was a hot LZ just two klicks north of the battalion staging area.

The throbbing pain in my head was increasing in intensity with the mechanical rattling of several hummers and amtracs as they ground their way up and over the rocky slope just fifty meters east of my fighting position. The pungent odor of diesel fuel was discomforting and brought a flare to my nostrils.

The corpsman had just finished dressing my lacerated upper arm when the company commander approached the foxhole. "How's it look?" the Captain asked as Doc gathered his first aid bag and climbed up out of the hole.

"About ten centimeters, maybe one deep. Probably need stitches once we all back on ship. Sir!" The corpsman appeared somewhat intimidated as he would not look at the C.O. directly in the eyes. Probably for good reason. Bennett was not overly fond of sailors, even navy corpsman. He was all U.S. Marine, all the time. And he was exactly what you would expect of a man in charge of a rifle company. Built like a brick shithouse, the seventeen year veteran owned the regimental record for push-ups, three hundred and forty two, in a single attempt. He was as intelligent as he was stern, and being a former enlisted man he had great empathy for his troops. Captain Michael Allen Bennett was the most highly regarded and respected company commander in the fifth marine regiment.

THE BOOK OF RICHARD

Bennett watched as I carefully pulled the sleeve of my camo blouse down over the blood soaked pressure bandage. He then focused onto the three inch, cigar-shaped blister that had formed across the cheek bone just below my right eye. "Damn Aites… You look like hell! Bayonet cut your arm and a spent cartridge charred your face." As I grinned in pain, my teeth were somewhat illuminated by the black soot of dust and gunpowder that coveted my face and lips. "What do you think about that weapon?" he asked, referring to the M249 light machine-gun that was sprawled across my lap.

"Jagged rock tore my arm…Red hot, spare barrel burnt my face…Weapon kicked my ass…Sir."

A rare smile came over the C.O.'s face. "Couldn't have kicked your ass too bad. Your platoon sergeant reported that you took out six enemy positions… single handedly. Good job Lance Corporal!" he then spit a large ball of tobacco juice and saliva into the South Korean soil.

"Thank you sir." I halfheartedly remarked.

"Looks like operation Colonel Blitz was a complete success!" a frail, whiny voice called out from somewhere behind the C.O. "The Major is well pleased!" The Chaplain added as he stepped alongside the Captain.

Bennett acted as if he didn't even acknowledge the young man's presence. "Aites, keep an eye on the wound. Check it so often and have the Doc change the dressing when need be. You don't need to take an infection home with you." Bennett said as he watched a trickle of blood dribble from under my sleeve forming a tiny pool on the back of my hand. He then spit another ball of juice onto the ground, barely missing the chaplain's left boot. "Any questions about the operation?" He grinned, apparently amused by the chaplain's clumsy attempt to sidestep the spittle.

"Well sir..." I replied as I recalled something that had been eating at me for most of the day. My mind returned to the previous dawn. The beach landing which met with little resistance and the long march through the village and into the Korean hillside.

"What is it?" Bennett demanded.

I quickly gathered my thoughts. "Well sir, it's been on my mind for most of the day." I paused to sip from a canteen of water. "Back at the village...an old farmer. My platoon trudged through his crop fields to avoid the mines and wire." I hesitated as I reflected upon the large, toothless yet sincere smile that covered his rugged, weathered face. The old Korean's home, a shanty, was not much larger than a porta-john. His only possessions were a few farming implements and a single pair of oxen. His only source of income were the two, four-acre fields which contained rice and barley. It was harvest time.

The C.O. appeared to be growing a bit impatient. Again I collected my thoughts. "That old farmer greeted us with a wave and a smile, all the while we were trampling his crops into the ground." A confused expression came across my sore face. "I don't understand it! Hell, I'd be one pissed off S.O.B.!"

Bennett slung his m16 rifle over his left shoulder. "I'll let the chaplain handle that one." He remarked as he proceeded towards the next fighting position to the west. I then focused onto the chaplain. Just as Bennett was one that a person might picture as a hard man in charge of a company of grunts, so to was Lt. Christopher Fischer as a military pastor. Tall with a meager build and almost completely bald, his slender, pale face was mounted with a pair of thick, black cat's eye glasses-- military issue of course. Physically, Lt. Fischer had the stamina of a sixty year old, emphysema patient.

THE BOOK OF RICHARD

It was also a well known fact that Fischer was nowhere to be found when it was time to participate in the regular twelve mile battalion march or five mile company run. Around noon chow however, he'd show up at the barracks, ready to console whoever needed it. Although physically meek, Fischer was as intelligent as any officer in the regiment. A recent graduate from the University of Illinois, he was a man of incredible insight. His predictions on the outcome of military operations, world events and even baseball games were uncanny. Many of the troops in my platoon addressed his by his nickname 'The Prophet'.

"Well, Lance Corporal Aites, try and look at it this way. Your farmer realizes that if the U.S. military was not here training, in his native land...Well, he and the few possessions that he does own would belong to the north. I think he understands that the loss of a few crops is a small price to pay for the freedom he possesses right now." It made sense. I nodded in appreciation of the chaplain's explanation.

Fischer then took up a crouching position alongside my hole. He removed his camo cap and scratched at his hairless, scaling head. "Can I talk to you for a minute?" He asked while replacing the cap.

I sighed in a bit of disagreement as I knew what was ahead. "Sir, if it's about reenlistment....the First Sergeant has been on my ass all week!"

Fischer appeared somewhat startled at my assumption. "Have you considered it?"

I acknowledged the chaplain's question with a slow nod. I then focused into the brilliant, glowing red orb that was inching its way below the jagged horizon.

As I peered deeper and deeper onto the fading sun, I reflected upon my life in and before the U.S. Marine Corps.

There were many plus and minuses to military service. And though I felt the positives out weighed the negatives, I had already made up my mind that my military career was over.

There was a time when I was content with the notion of being a 'lifer'. My father and an uncle had served in the Marines during the Vietnam era. I became brainwashed as a child because during many drunken stupors, my father made it clear to me that the Marine Corps would make me into a man. And being raised in a small, rural Pennsylvania oil town--my ambition was modest and my goals, simple.

Yet my enlistment helped open my eyes to life beyond the doldrums of small town living. My transfer to Camp Pendleton introduced me to the wonders of Los Angeles, Hollywood and San Diego. When not in the field training, I was in the hottest nightclubs in the area, fraternizing with women and consuming vast quantities of alcoholic beverages.

Once a shy, bucked tooth kid from a timid little town, now I had a tan, some muscle and a face that was compared to that of a popular pop singer at the time, George Michael. I was confident, and arrogant. One time, during a 96 hour liberty, I was offered a job in a prominent L.A. night club as a Chippendale dancer. The owner offered me a salary which was almost five times the amount was making annually in the military. I turned it down however because I was homophobic at the time and this man was a well known homosexual.

I liked the club scene. I saw great amounts of money being made and beautiful women being bought. Woman, money and fun, success was almost certainly around the corner and my new found ambition was drawing me away from the sense of duty which had owned me from childhood.

"Yes sir, I have thought about it a lot. I love being a grunt. The field, attacking and defending objectives. The rifle range. Jumping out of helicopters and repelling down the side of three hundred foot mountain slopes. That's what I'm about." I replied as I slapped a large, centipede that was meandering its way up my injured arm.

"Then why not re-up?" Fischer asked as he quickly shifted his weight to the left to avoid the airborne insect.

"Politics, inspections…I just need to move on…" I replied as the chaplain's attention was averted to the corpsman standing somewhere near the command post.

"Chaplain Fischer! Chow is ready!" Doc hollered while shaking a large, golden bell he received as a gift from one of the local farmers.

Fischer immediately stood to his feet. "The captain has allowed for a prayer service tonight around 1900 hours at the C.P. Tonight's topic will cover the book of revelation. Can I expect you there?"

I removed a M.R.E. from my winter pack and a K-BAR knife from the cartridge belt. "Don't have much to pray for Sir. Except maybe all those poor women I plan on a fornicatin' with when we get back to Cali!" I replied with a smirk as I slit open the brown plastic pouch containing the food ration.

The chaplain grinned as though not amused. A serious expression overcame his mouse-like face. "Ten years down the road, a day will come when you will need the Lord! Believe me, you'll be a calling."

CHAPTER TWO

Nearly four months later, three young Marines climbed into a convertible, leaving Camp Pendleton behind and making their way south into San Diego. After spending the past five days in the field during another rugged training exercise, a weekend liberty was granted to everyone in the battalion. Everybody that could, left the base to catch up on more recreational activities--namely-partying and women.

On the following Sunday morning, after two nights of intense club hoppin', myself, LCPL Hodson and LCPL Stillman stood on the parking lot outside our hotel room. It was brisk morning but the blazing orange sun that was climbing up into the horizon was rapidly warming the thin, salted air. Leaning up against Hodson's brand new, candy apple red, Mustang, we were contemplating what to do before the day was out and having to return to Camp Pendleton.

Our cash resources nearly exhausted, we stared down the busy four lane avenue in which the hotel sat and watched as early morning passer-bys made their way to the local beach. It was a young, single man's paradise, watching attractive young women clad in dark tans and thongs, speed by our position in fast little mazdas or sporty little convertibles.

While Hodson tossed a headful of ideas our way, we suddenly observed a man appear, seemingly out of nowhere. Caucasion and of modest build, his brown, shoulder length hair was matted and filthy. His face was partially covered in a black substance that appeared to be of petroleum base, probably motor oil. He approached us from the middle of the street while cars swerved around him to avoid making him a part of the roadway. His unusual attire consisted of a heavy, flannel shirt and weathered, torn 501 blue jeans. He was toting a motorcycle helmet in his scathed and bloodied left hand.

"Where in the hell did he come from?" Hodson asked as the injured man made his way across the heavy traffic flow and onto the lot.

"I don't know! It's like the S.O.B. came out of nowhere!" Stillman replied as the stranger approached us and halted several feet from our position. A look of despair owned his face as the smell of body odor and musty clothing owned his form. He looked me directly in the eyes as he extended his free hand towards me in a non-verbal cry for help. In a timid yet sincere voice he told us that he was involved in a serious motorcycle accident on Beachfront Blvd. He advised us that he was broke and homeless and needed a few dollars for gas so that he could be on his way. "I beg of you," he finished.

Though most of our money was spent, I was aware that both Stillman and Hodson had quite a bit more money than I. Yet I also knew that Stillman was some what tight with his cash and Hodson was downright stingy. Knowing that what little cash we had left was meant for on final party in the afternoon, I expected a harsh response to the stranger's request from my fellow jarheads.

"Get the hell out of here! You're not getting' any money out of us you friggin' beggar!" Hodson shouted.

"Go get a damned job like the rest of us asshole!" Stillman added. The man did not budge as he remained focused upon me.

"I said get the hell out of here!" Hodson demanded as he raised a clenched fist into the air in an attempt to strike the meager man. I immediately intercepted Hodson's falling forearm, clutching his left wrist in the air above the stranger's bowing head. The young Marine yanked his arm away from me in hostility.

The anguish on the stranger's face was overwhelming and for the first time in a long while, compassion engulfed my cold, hardened soul. I reached into the front pocket of my stone washed Levi's and removed a small bundle of crumpled cash. As I unraveled the money, I counted twelve dollars--a five and seven ones.

"Aites! Don't tell me you're going to give him money. You barely have enough to get yourself a few drinks at the beach." Hodson reminded me. Without acknowledging him, I removed the five dollar bill from the bundle and handed it to the stranger. He grinned as though he were in severe pain and hesitantly took the bill from my hand.

"Blessed are you my friend." He said quietly as I peered into the deepness of his unusually dark eyes. Words could not describe what I saw as I focused through the vastness of a wisdom I could not comprehend.

"Think maybe you need an ambulance?" I asked as I stepped back into reality.

"Your kindness was enough." He replied as he crumpled the bill in the palm of his uninjured hand, turned and proceeded back towards the street.

Hodson and Stillman laughed sarcastically. "He just took you for five bucks!"

"I can't believe you fell for that bullshit!" Hodson shouted.

"He's on his way to the liquor store to get himself a pint of whiskey, you dumbass!" Stillman added. "That's alright! But when we get to the beach, I ain't lending you a dime."

Before stepping back into the busy roadway, the stranger turned and faced me once again. "Join your family in St. Louis, and many blessings will be bestowed upon you!" He shouted as he stepped into the street.

"That crazy S.O.B. is going to get leveled!" Stillman said as he bent down to tie his shoe.

"I thought your family is in Pennsylvania?" Hodson asked me.

"They are. I don't know what in the hell that guy's talking about!" I replied as the three of us focused back out onto the avenue. The stranger was gone. Just as he appeared, he disappeared before our very eyes.

"Too hell with this crazy shit! Let's get a drink." Hodson declared as we climbed into the car and headed for the beach.

Three weeks after our weekend liberty in San Diego, I received a phone call from my parents. My father had been laid off from his job at the mill and was forced to seek employment elsewhere. The unemployment rate was extremely high in northwestern Pennsylvania at the time as jobs are few and far between. My father, mother and two brothers packed up and moved to the Midwest where jobs were abundant. They settled in St. Louis.

In the spring of 1990 I received my honorable discharge from the USMC. After four years of spit and polish, pounding the dirt and working every shit detail pushed off onto me, I was ready for civilian life.

Yet I was humbled to learn that Hollywood and the city of angels was not for me. A handsome face was a dime a dozen and my acting ability was zero to none.

It wasn't long after my discharge that I flew to St. Louis to give the gateway city a try.

As for being a blessing, my family struggled as we worked minimum wage jobs in fast-food joints and unskilled labor billets. In 1993 we were twice moved from the bitter waters of the great flood while at the same time, I was battling a mild case of alcoholism.

In 1994 the dark cloud which I had helped to create, lifted, and as the sky opened, light again filtered into my darkened soul. The call of duty was urgent and the Police Academy became my only hope. For the first time in five years, I was committed.

THE BOOK OF RICHARD

CHAPTER THREE: Summer 1998

"Adam units, assault with a knife, 8405 Alderaan Drive, apartment one-north. THE SUSPECT IS STILL IN THE BUILDING!" the squelch from the radio was almost deafening as I yanked the mic from its magnetic dash mount.

"Adam six is clear and enroute!" I answered before tossing the mic across the dashboard in a bit of frustration. "Seven o'clock in the goddamn morning!" I shouted upon wasting a half cup of hot coffee out the car window and engaging the emergency lights of the Ford police interceptor.

Hurriedly making my way through the congested, early morning traffic, I arrived on the scene three minutes later. A tall, thin African-American woman was standing at the front door of the section eight, apartment building. She was screaming hysterically and her white nightgown was covered in blood.

"That son of a bitch tried to kill me! He cut off my f___in' hand!" She screamed while clutching onto her bloodied, right forearm. "Help me officer!" she pleaded as I approached her. I quickly examined the bleeding wound.

" The paramedics will be here any minute." I reassured her. I then focused onto the apartment building. "Is the guy who cut you... Is he still in the apartment?"

"Yes he is! His name is Jeffrey and he's a goddamn lunatic! He got a big knife and a mental condition!" The victim hollered in pain. She then pulled her left hand away from the wound and pointed to the first floor apartment located on the north side of the building. At that moment my patrol supervisor arrived.

"Corporal Carll! She needs a pressure bandage and a good wrap until the medics arrive!" I shouted as I proceeded to the first floor, apartment door. Carll immediately removed the first-aid kit from the trunk of his patrol car. I drew my duty pistol and held it down at my right side. I then inched my way to the door and began knocking on its thick wooden exterior.

I double checked the safety switch on the handgun and identified myself as a police officer. After several attempts with no response, I focused on Carll, who was dressing the woman's severed hand. "I'm going in!" I announced as I raised my right knee. Carll nodded in approval. With two swift kicks, the deadbolt assembly dismantled from the door and frame and bounced across the wooden living room floor. With pistol raised to eye level and laser sight engaged, I cautiously entered into the semidarkened living quarters.

Several pieces of furniture were overturned, definite signs of a struggle. As I stepped over and around the obstacles I observed and large pool of blood on the floor in front of a small coffee table. The table appeared undisturbed as several razor blades, a small compact mirror and other pieces of drug paraphernalia lay strewn across its surface. As the laser sight on my pistol made it's way across the far wall, I observed several bloodied handprints running across the light exterior. I moved across the room and found a light switch but it was to now avail as there were no bulbs in the overhead fixtures.

I made my way into the kitchen where I observed a large freezer bag with a white in color substance resting beside a digital scale on the counter beside the sink. I recognized the powder as cocaine.

Upon exiting the kitchen, I heard a loud thud come from the rear of the apartment. It sounded as if someone were attempting to break a window. I stepped into a small, hazy corridor where the smell of cigarette smoke filled my nostrils. As I proceeded down the darkened hallway I found a back bedroom door standing partially open. This was the origin of the sound that I had heard while in the kitchen. Upon pushing the door completely open, I was startled by a sudden movement in the far corner of the room. The nickel-sized red dot from the laser sight came to rest, center mass, on the figure of a man standing in the corner.

Though I could barely make out his face, I could see into his cold, wicked eyes. He was a small man but the large ginzu style, butcher knife made him a dangerous adversary. "Drop the knife, and raise your hands above your head!" I demanded as the laser sight bounced up and down the man's upper torso. The suspect appeared to ignore my demand as he continued to stare right through me. "You see that bright red dot resting upon your sternum?" The suspect suddenly focused down onto the dot. "In about two seconds, a forty caliber, jacketed hollow-point is going to rip through your sternum, penetrating your chest cavity and exploding you friggin' heart! You'll drop where you stand. No bullshit! It's not a good day to die, JEFFREY!" The suspect continued to focus on the motionless red orb.

A moment later, the knife fell to the floor and the suspect surrendered. Within the hour, the suspect was sitting in the interrogation room with myself and Detective Ronald Webber. Once the suspect was advised of his Miranda rights, his first request was a cigarette. After taking several hits from the cancer stick, Jeffrey told us that he wished to make a statement and did not care to have a lawyer present.

"The voices told me to kill her. We was smokin' crack and the voices came back. They told me to cut her up, and kill her." He paused to take another puff from the cigarette. "I tried to cut her throat but she wrestled free. She's one lucky bitch. She should be dead because the voices usually make me strong!" Jeffrey then broke eye contact with Detective Webber and focused into the dingy white ceiling above our heads. "She's one lucky bitch!"

It was later determined that the suspect was a manic depressant with a cocaine habit. "That's not a very good combination, is it Jeffrey? Cocaine and anti-depressants." Webber noted. The suspect just nodded. As I escorted Jeffrey out of the interrogation room, Webber halted us momentarily. A somewhat puzzled look was on the detective's face. "Just curious Jeffrey. Did the voices tell you to hurt Officer Aites? When he came into your apartment?"

The suspect turned and faced Webber. He removed his gaze from the floor. "Yes." He responded, looking the detective in the eyes.

"How come you were able to ignore them this time?" Jeffrey then focused onto me. He briefly looked me over, from head to toe. At that time I was still in my late twenties and a model policeman. Almost six feet tall with an athletic build, I was a solid two hundred pounds. My bright green eyes and chiseled, tanned face gave me the look of both intelligence and confidence.

"Well?" Webber asked impatiently. Jeffrey focused back onto the detective.

"Some people are protected from the voices. I looked into his eyes and saw...."Jeffrey hesitated in a blank stare.

"Saw what?" Webber demanded.

"He would have killed me." The suspect stated as he turned and was escorted out the door.

I transported the suspect to the county jail where he was to be held pending warrant application. An hour later, I left the prosecuting attorney's office with a freshly signed warrant in hand. I made my way back to the jail where I served the warrant and advised the suspect of the $75,000.00 bond. Upon being informed of the enormous bond, a blank, cold stare came over Jeffrey. I recognized it from the apartment.

As I turned to leave, Jeffrey hollered, "We're coming to get you motherf___er! If not you, than your child that is soon to come!" This startled me. I spun around and faced Jeffrey who was clutching onto the thick, cold bars of the heavy steel door.

"How did you know my wife was with child?" I demanded.

Jeffrey smiled sinisterly. "The voices told me, you fool! They tell me everything you f____in' jarhead!"

"Go to hell!" I replied as I turned and followed the heavy set correctional officer to the massive cell block door.

"We'll see you and your infant son there, mother f___er!" Jeffrey shouted in disgust as the correctional officer slammed the door shut.

Later that afternoon, exhausted, I found myself standing upon a great, asphalt plain. I looked in all directions and found that the mega-parking lot extended beyond the horizon. Waves of steam arose from the hot tar-like surface which was saturated from a recent rain. The sky was thick and gray with heavy thunderheads rolling in from the west. Beads of sweat formed on my forehead as my navy blue uniform was absorbing much of the unbearable summer-time heat.

A sudden chill overcame me as I became disorientated about my location. "Where in the hell am I?" I asked myself while wiping the sweat from my brow. I then reached for my hand-held walkie in an attempt to contact the dispatcher, but the radio was missing from its case.

I was then overwhelmed with the feeling of being alone before I heard something from behind me. It was like a quiet voice, a whisper calling out to me. I couldn't understand what was being said but I could now feel a presence closing in. I turned and no one was there. I then became frightened when I realized that the invisible presence was evil. I reached for my duty weapon, but it too was missing.

Suddenly the sky opened up and a great pillar of brilliant light broke through the clouds and engulfed my trembling form. I was the knocked violently to the hard, asphalt surface. I couldn't move as I peered into the beautiful light above. A feeling of great joy and well being overcame me. The fear of being alone fled as did the evil presence it accompanied, for I was no longer alone. "Of whose works shall you be committed?" A mighty voice, greater that thunder, said from up above.

"Wake up Rich!" Officer Howard said as he shook my left should. I opened my eyes and focused upon the gray ceiling about. I sat up on the bench while rubbing my eyes and focusing on Howard who was standing at the far end of the locker room. "Go home and get some sleep. You had a long day, with that stabbing and the warrant application." Howard said as he slammed the locker door shut before securing the lock.

"What time is it?" I asked.

"Three-thirty, shift change was an hour ago." Howard advised as he exited the locker room.

"My wife's going to kick my ass!" I mumbled upon leaving the station two minutes later.

It was an unusually mild summer in St. Louis but the murder rate was climbing much faster than the midday thermometer. The number of homicides in the city were leaps and bounds ahead of those in Chicago and even LA. We were on pace to set a record as the post dispatch and local news agencies continually reminded us.

Fortunately, it was relatively quiet in the small, north county community in which I patrolled. Only a single tally represented my little sector in the growing list of victims. Other than responding on an occasional call for police or making an arrest on the street, I basically watched over the citizens as they played out their everyday roles in society.

Most would rise early, shuffling their half awakened children into cozy, air-conditioned station wagons or bullet shaped mini-vans. Fathers and mothers alike, dispatching their little ones to daycare or the sitters before mustering into the office or onto the assembly line for another long day ahead.

The retired folk were early risers to. They spent their days tending to the tiny gardens and lush, green lawns that were prospering in the comfortable, humidity free afternoons.

The smaller portion of the community's population did not rise until much later. For these were the lazy unemployed, cotton-mouthed alcoholics and the 'self employed' as they addressed themselves. Most of this kind could be found crawling out of their holes around the same time that the working class was eating lunch. Later on in the afternoon you could find them kicking back on someone's front porch while sipping on cheap beer or gin and smoking dope. They despised work and were riding the easy life as their habits were supported by the check they received at the beginning of each month from the government. At night and into the wee hours of the morning many of society's little ulcers peddled their goods to addicts or anyone searching for a quick fix.

THE BOOK OF RICHARD

When I looked upon the faces of the early risers I could see in their welcoming expressions that they liked what I represented. Yet the vampires' expressions were sour and scornful, for they hated me and those just like me. Though I was not the wooden stake in their hearts, I was at times, a thorn in their sides. The constitution all too often protected their illegal affairs, and they know their rights well, even though they cared nothing for the law.

Yet as all good Police Officers know, you don't take it personal. You keep an open mind and try to put yourself in their shoes. Many are victims of their upbringing and environment. The officer must also realize that he is just as human under the badge and accepting that his authority is limited keeps things in perspective. I read a bumper sticker one that said 'God hates sin but loves the Sinner'. A good motto to live by as a law enforcement officer.

When the midnight shift came around, quiet became placid and the shifts seemed to drag on endlessly. It did however give one a lot of time to think and I was able to keep an accurate count down of the days leading to my child's birth. It also gave me time to reflect on the former things and events that were stored within my short and long term memory banks. There was one event that I couldn't seem to shake. I kept recalling the statements made by the 'crack head' with the knife. I was still somewhat rattled over what he had said about the 'voices' while at the county jail. I would eventually convince myself that the suspect overhead me speaking to another Officer about my wife's pregnancy and put two and two together. The only problem is that I did not recall mentioning it to anyone while the suspect was in my custody.

RICHARD W. AITES

The summer was coming to a close as the school year began once again. Something was stirring as it had been quiet for much to long. I could feel the tension almost as clearly as one could smell autumn in the air.

THE BOOK OF RICHARD

CHAPTER FOUR: FALL, 1998

The lecture was coming to a close when the call came out. The plastic dixie cup that my partner was utilizing to demonstrate the art of lifting latent prints to the fourth grade mystery club fell to the floor as he rushed for the exit door. After acknowledging the call, the dispatcher advised that the OBS subject was barricaded in the house, armed with a rifle and handgun, and was threatening to kill the neighbors.

The wail of the siren was deafening as it rocketed off the thick, concrete library wall. Two seconds later, my partner swerved off of the lot and was destined for Forest Avenue. I turned over the ignition on the Ford police interceptor and cranked up the volume on the oldies station. Before exiting the library parking lot I flipped up a couple of toggle switches on the center console box engaging emergency lights and siren. With lights a flare and a blaring siren announcing my approach, I was on Forest Avenue in a mere two minutes. Adrenaline was rushing like fire through my veins as I grabbed the radio mic and alerted the dispatcher of my arrival. There was a loud squelch of radio interference before my partner came over the air. "Adam six, you need to clock off Forest at Walton Road to keep all traffic from approaching east! This guy's a maniac and could start shooting any time!"

"Clear." I answered as I spun the car around blocking off the narrow roadway.

I locked the vehicle up and dashed two hundred meters up Forest until I reached my partner's car. Parked almost directly in front of the suspect's house, Paul was kneeling behind the right front quarter-panel with a 12-gauge shotgun propped on the hood and its muzzle pointed at the front door.

A loud metallic banging came from inside the house. "What in the hell is that?" I asked.

"The S.O.B is slamming the butt of his rifle up against the front door." Paul answered. The door began to vibrate from the beating.

"Come on in you coward sons a bitches! Ain't you got the f____n' guts?' A deep hostile voice yelled from behind the door. "I'll kill all you bastards!"

By this time there were nearly ten units from surrounding municipalities on the scene. The radio silence was broken by the voices of the scene commander. "One of you guys to the south needs to cautiously respond to the house just east of the suspect's, have the residents...have the residents find a secure position in the basement."

As several officers began taking covered position surrounding the suspect's house, I told my partner to cover me as I sprinted to the neighbor's front porch. I then crawled onto the porch and duck walked to the front door. A young woman responded to the door. An alarming look came over her expressions she observed me kneeling in an attempt to keep a low profile below the three foot brick wall.

The woman quickly gathered her children and rushed them into the basement. Before exiting the porch, I peered through a window located on the eastside of the suspect's house. I watched as he continued to pound the buttstock of the rifle against the front door. I could see his entire profile through the window. A big, burly man, rage owned his expression. "Come on in you no good motherf_____s! I'll kill you all!" He shouted as I made my way off of the porch and assisted two other officers in securing the northeast corner of the perimeter.

A half an hour later it was dark. The suspect, who I discovered was named 'John', had made his way to the enclosed back porch and was standing at the top step. With a semi-automatic pistol in one hand and a bottle of Seagrams rum in the other, John took up a seat on the step. The thud from his heavy frame falling upon the step activated the motion sensored spot light which illuminated John's upper torso and a small portion of the fenced in back yard.

As John placed the pistol down beside his right leg, I observed the .223 caliber rifle leaning up against the porch wall directly to the suspect's left. The rifle was easily within his reach. The suspect swished the rum around the half empty bottle before taking a quick swill.

"What's wrong...Ain't none of you got any balls? Show yourselves you friggin' cowards!" he demanded before taking another mouthful of Seagrams. The officer just south of my position advised me that John was an alcoholic and was on anti-depressants for a severe case of manic depression. I was further advised that John had attempted suicide just three weeks earlier.

"Great, suicide by cop!" I remarked as an officer hidden behind the garage just north of the suspect's house attempted to negotiate with him.

"May be. But I think he wants to take a couple of us with him!" the officer replied.

John then reached back down and recovered the shiny, stainless steel pistol. He held it in his lap. "Put your weapon down and come off the steps with your hands in the air!" the negotiating officer demanded.

"Go to hell asshole!" John answered as the officer illuminated the suspects rugged, bearded face with a powerful mag-lite. Angered, John reached behind him, gathering the rifle and holding it at his left side. "Turn off that goddamned flashlight or I'll start shootin'!" Several service pistols were raised with sights aligned on John's big, upper torso.

"You start shooting and you'll die!" The officer from behind the garage shouted as John stood holding a rifle in one hand and a pistol in the other.

Though several handguns and shotguns honed in on the mass called John, fenced in backyard was a barrier which separated us a good fifty meters from the suspect. The only weapon truly effective at that range was the rifle that was held by John. The tact team had been notified but their ETA was another twenty minutes and time was running out.

Seeing that the negotiations were not working, I made my way from my covered position behind the neighbor's house and took up a kneeling position in the middle of the rear yard. My only cover was the darkness of night. "What are you doing?" An officer asked form his position behind the cellar wall.

"I'm going to try to establish a rapport with this asshole." I replied as I holstered me service pistol.

As John slammed the bolt home on the rifle, the clatter of a cartridge being flung upon the sidewalk below the steps brought a profound expression across his numb, forbidding face. Apparently he forgot that the rifle had been loaded or he was attempting to be intimidating, regardless, it worked. The officer with the maglite immediately withdrew into an adjacent yard. "You friggin' cowards afraid to show yourselves? You all hidin' behind trees and garages, like gaddamn cowards!"

The loud static of radio interference caught my attention as well as John's as the dispatcher advised all units to switch to the riot channel. I immediately turned down the volume on my handheld unit while at the same time, clicking the channel knob to six. John picked up on the static and my movement as he placed the rifle down across his lap and focused upon me, a ghost in the darkness. "If my guns won't get ya! My dog will! He's trained to eat cops!" John hollered as he raised his forearm above his brow in an effort to get a visual on my kneeling outline.

"What's wrong John?" I asked as John stood to his feet clutching the rifle at his side.

"I don't like to talk to someone unless I know their name and can see their face!" he shouted in disgust.

"Rich!" I replied as I inched my way to a picnic table that sat but twenty meters from John's position. The dispatcher's voice again came over the radio, only this time the volume was low enough that it didn't alarm our intoxicated suspect. She advised that the tactical units ETA was still twenty to twenty-five minutes.

"Shit man! Be careful!" Another officer shouted from somewhere behind me. As I sat down on the table, my face and upper torso became partially illuminated by the spotlight above John's head.

"Come a little closer!" he demanded in a seemingly sinister voice before reaching for the bottle of Seagrams and downing another unhealthy mouthful.

"I'll come a little closer as long as you promise not to shoot my ass!" I moved to within fifteen meters.

"Oh! I ain't makin' no promises. Just keep your hands away from that holster!" he ordered as he pointed the muzzle of the rifle in my direction. I was so close I could smell the liquor about his breath.

"You're an insane S.O.B. ! I could kill you right now!" He said as his trigger finger cradled the half inch piece of steel that was the only significance between my life and death.

I swallowed the lump in my throat. "Listen John! No one is gonna die tonight! My first baby is due on Christmas Eve and

I'm going to be there to greet the little shit!" I paused to wipe the sweat from my brow. "Even if you did shoot me...I ain't gonna die anyway...I cant afford to, so let's quit talkin' about this shootin' bullshit and get to some worthwhile conversation. Why are you having such a bad day?"

John removed his finger from the trigger and took another swallow of rum. At that moment it appeared as though he relinquished the fire from his eyes. "I don't know Rich. You ain't never had a bad day?" He replied.

"Sure I have! Are you married John?"

A puzzled look came over John's face. "No! but what in the hell does that have to do with anything?"

"Well I am. And believe me...everydays a bad friggin' day!" John laughed at my response.

"Congratulations on your baby!" John uttered as the hostility seemed to subside into the darkness of the night. "Tell me Rich...what is the meaning of life? Because tonight, I was planning on ending mine!"

"Hell John! There isn't a son of a bitch out here, who hasn't thought about sticking a gun to their head at one time or another! If they tell you any different, than their full of shit! Everybody has problems!"

"Wait a second!" John interrupted as he raised the bottle to his mouth and swigged another mouthful.

He then wiped his burled forearm across his mouth. "My friggin' psychiatrist can't even tell me the meaning of life! Can you? A low life cop?" John again raised the almost empty bottle to his mouth.

There was a brief moment of silence as I collected my thoughts. "I doubt that I have the answer that your looking for, but I'll tell you how I look at it...if you'll hear me out!"

"Since you're the only one with any balls…I guess I'll listen to what you've got to say!" He said loudly in an attempt to humiliate the audience he so much despised.

"I look at it this way. Life is like a book. It's got good chapters and some bad ones. It's got a beginning and an end. John! If you close the book in the middle somewhere, just toss it aside! Well, you'll never know how it's going to end!"

John appeared somewhat amused by the speech. Go on! He demanded.

"John, you're the author of this book. You're the one telling the story. Don't close the book know! If you do, you'll never know how it ended!" A confused and contorted expression came over his suddenly somber face. "What I'm trying to say is that you need to grow old. Watch your children and theirs make it in this world before you leave. I believe it is here that you will find meaning!"

John stood to his feet before shoving the empty bottle in my direction. "I like you Rich. Come, let's have a drink together!" At about the same time, the tactical unit was setting up position along the west wall. They were clad in thick helmets with face shields and body armor from head to toe. Blending in with the shadows, the group of four men were armed with semi-automatic rifles and concussion grenades.

A small amount of friction broke through the radio silence. "We've got way too much ground to cover here. We need to get him down from the porch and away from those weapons." A quiet voice announced over the riot channel. I had the volume switch on the lowest possible setting and fortunately, John was unable to hear the message.

"If you come down off the porch and meet me at the base of the steps, I'll have a drink with you!" John smirked before downing the last swallow of liquor left in the bottle. He then

THE BOOK OF RICHARD

tossed the empty bottle onto the yard below. "I'll be right back!" he said as he turned, entered into the doorway and proceeded back into the house carrying the rifle at his side.

"Shit!" I hollered after realizing how dangerous he was now that we had lost visual contact. A few moments later John returned with a brand new bottle of rum. He twisted off the cap utilizing his large, tarnished teeth.

As he raised the bottle to his mouth, he paused, bringing the bottle back down and resting it upon his swollen hip. "Okay! So I come down the steps. Then what? I get arrested! No friggin' way!" John announced as he quickly removed the bottle from his hip and slammed another mouthful.

"Listen John! I've kept my end of the bargain. Now meet me halfway. I'll move towards the fence, if you start makin' your way down the steps. Deal!" I then foolishly made my way closer to the armed man.

John was not amused. "I know that if come down these f___in' steps to bring you a drink, you're gonna try and arrest me!"

"Ah John! I'm not going to blow smoke up your ass. I will be takin' you into protective custody. I don't want to see you or anyone else get hurt tonight. As far as being arrested! You haven't hurt anyone tonight, except maybe your damned liver. There are no charges. So let's quit the bullshit and have a drink. I could sure use one about now."

John laid the rifle down across the top step. He then focused back upon me. "Rich! If I come down there, you'd better help me finish off this bottle!" He then lowered his right foot on a step below.

"I'll have one or two drinks with you, but that's about all I can have." I replied as John clumsily made his way to the bottom step.

"One or two drinks!" John smirked. "Let me guess! You can't drink because you're on duty." He added.

"No, not quite! It's because I'm getting' close to going home, and if my wife smells liquor on my breath. Well John, if you don't shoot my ass, she will!" John laughed as he staggered onto the concrete slab below the steps. I was not standing at the fence a mere ten meters from the mass known as John. Only now, his only weapon was a liter boot of Seagram. As John staggered towards me, the faint squelch of my walkie was followed by the words, "We're going to take him." Before John could fully extend his right arm to hand me the bottle, a massive shadow of men converged upon us from behind.

"Get down! Get down!" They shouted in desperation as John was immediately knocked to the ground. I jumped over the fence and quickly drew my weapon as John struggled with the tact members. "You no good cowards! Can't take me one on one!" John bellowed as a pile of bodies attempted to keep his pinned on the ground. The struggle lasted for what appeared to be an eternity before the massive hulk of intoxicated redneck was handcuffed.

While returning my weapon to my holster, a loud crash came from the back porch area. I then observed a large dog, a boxer, come bounding down the steps. Easily seventy pounds with teeth that resemble polished daggers, the animal made his way into the yard and leaped onto the pile of me that were trying to get his owner to his feet. The dog lunged at the members tearing away some of their protective gear as they tried to lift John's passive resistant mass from off the ground.

Myself and another officer grabbed the animal's two back legs and were able to momentarily pull him away from the team. But the dog broke free just seconds later and lunged at me. I was able to kick him back the first time with a good stout blow to the chest. The dog immediately recovered to his feet. The animal's eyes appeared red with anger as it clicked its inch-long canines together. I again drew my weapon from my holster and activated the laser sight. The dog snarled with aggression as the bright red dot found the center of its darkened outline. A second later, the shadow lunged for my waist and I instinctively fired off a round. The blast from the round brought an eerie silence to the backyard. The animal gave out a loud howl and urinated on the ground below, before hobbling out onto the driveway and collapsing.

John was secured in an ambulance and transported to an area hospital for evaluation. The dog was later taken to the vet by a friend of John's family.

The tact team searched the back porch and house and found several handguns and rifles, fully loaded. Apparently, John was prepared for war.

Several officers commended me for my courage and effort in facing the armed man and gaining his trust. "You've got a baby on the way and you took a risk like that. You're either stupid, nuts or the most courageous S.O.B. I've ever met in my life!" One officer remarked.

"Stupid." I acknowledged as another member of the tact team pulled me aside. He told me that had I not been able to talk John into coming off the porch, there surely would have been a shoot-out. He appeared a bit disappointed when he told me that I saved John's life.

CHAPTER FIVE: December, 1998

    Several days before my wife discovered that she was pregnant in the later part of March, I had mentioned to her that it would be nice to gave a baby by Christmas. Before the discovery my wife had become discouraged because we have been trying for several months and it appeared as though child bearing was eluding us. Two days later the O.B. determined that the baby's due date was December 24th. An early ultra sound confirmed the doctor's belief.

    Wende was never a smoker and seldom partook in the consumption of alcoholic beverages. During the pregnancy she avoided alcohol completely and even became cognizant of any caffeine intake. While I jogged around the track, Wende walked, often covering three miles.

    In the fourth month of her pregnancy, the ultra sound revealed a healthy fetus. Deciding to be old fashioned, we refused to learn the sex of our child. An old wive's tale about the heartbeat and the way Wende was carrying the baby confirmed our belief that in December, Rheanna Taylor or Taylor Renee, would be our first born.

    The pregnancy went well for the first eight and a half months. Regular visits to the doctor revealed a healthy fetus and several childbirth preparation classes built our confidence. At the doctor's direction, my wife began to monitor the fetal movements (kicks and punches) at 28 weeks. The fetus was very active and she would usually feel ten required movements within the first ten minutes of the allotted two-hour time limit. That was however, until the evening of December 9th.

    I had just arrived home from my college class to find Wende in a grave state of concern. She informed me that she hadn't felt the baby move all day, nor had she felt a movement during the allotted two hours. I assumed that because the fetus was resting lower toward the birth canal and because of the nearness of the due date, that the baby's movements were more restricted and less pronounced. This theory however did not comfort my wife and she immediately contacted the doctor.

Within an hour, Wende Aites was given an epidural and prepped for an emergency C-section. An ultra sound revealed that the baby was under severe distress. I couldn't help but feel saddened for my wife as she went through the discomfort of the unwanted epidural. The look on her face as she was made aware of the pending operation and the baby's deteriorating condition almost brought me to my knees, yet I needed to remain strong for her sake.

The operation was performed and the baby was taken at 12:42am on December 10th. Twelve hours later, the baby stopped breathing and was rushed to Cardinal Glennon Children's Hospital where he was stabilized and diagnosed with a deadly blood disorder.

While Wende was recovering from the operation, the doctors informed us about the purpose of the emergency C-section and of the baby's complications. The family doctor said that there was no medical explanation for what had happened. Apparently during the latter part of the pregnancy, the placenta had ceased to develop, which created a great amount of stress to the fetus. When the fetus was not receiving the oxygen it needed, the baby's body began producing an over abundance of red blood cells to compensate.

Once born, the baby's blood was so thick in red blood cells that it created a congested and sluggish circulatory system which would later cause respiratory distress, nearly costing the baby his life.

RICHARD W. AITES

Later that evening, while driving along highway forty into downtown St. Louis, the images of my newborn son kept racing across my mind. Frail and barely five pounds, his tiny body was as red as a ripe tomato, a symptom of his illness. As Christmas music hymned over the local 'oldies' station, I reflected upon the urgency in the doctor's eyes and voices when my son was nearly unresponsive during the apgar testing. I then recalled the most devastating moment in my life. I had just arrived home from St. Joseph's Hospital only to receive a phone call informing me that the baby had stopped breathing. Upon receiving such news, I fell to my knees. In my eyes, the baby was lost.

I vaguely remember driving like a maniac to get back to the hospital and arriving to find my wife sobbing in grief and the infant being stabilized in an incubator type contraption with more than a dozen tubes and wires running in and out of his tiny nostrils and mouth, hands and feet, in an attempt to keep him alive. Not two minutes after my arrival, the baby was rushed by ambulance to Cardinal Glennon.

Upon exiting onto Grand Blvd. I followed the narrow but busy roadway about a mile before pulling onto the Cardinal Glennon lot. A few minutes later I stepped out of the elevator and onto the fourth floor. Following a coupe of wall markers, I proceeded down a lengthy corridor until coming upon a large steel door marked N.I.C.U. A LPN demonstrated the art of scrubbing down before leading me into a vast room where several babies were lying in clear, plastic bassinets and incubator type contraptions, similar to the one my son was transported in from St. Joseph's.

The room was noisy with the racket of fussing infants and the mechanical chimes and blips of monitors. I followed the nurse to the center of the ward where Chayce was sleeping in

THE BOOK OF RICHARD

an open bassinet. This new father's heart sank into his gut upon observing the sleeping infant hooked up to oxygen to aid in breathing. Still as red as ketchup, several pieces of tape dotted his tiny chest to secure the minute sensors that were recording his vital signs.

Tears filled my eyes as I focused down onto the tiny fragment of a human being. "Would you like to hold him?" the nurse asked. Nodding in silent agreement, the nurse gently placed the infant in my arms. A tear made its way down across my cheek and over my chin before falling upon the baby's tiny forehead. "Well look at that." The nurse said as the baby flinched and briefly opened his eyes as if focusing on his father above. For the first time in twenty-four hours, a smile came over my face.

After spending two hours at Cardinal Glennon, I drove back to St. Joseph's to be with Wende.

As I entered the hospital's main entrance I observed a wall sign marked 'chapel'. Extremely down about my child's seemingly hopeless situation, I followed the arrow pointing left and proceeded into a small, semi-darkened room that owned but two dozen benches. A large, golden cross was gleaming with candlelight as it was mounted on the far wall several feet above the layman's podium. The cross depicted a wonderful image of Christ.

The chapel was empty and the beautiful cross seemed to call out to me, silently. Therefore I made my way down the center aisle and around the podium where I stood below the cross of gold. It had been quite some time since I last spoke to God, in sincerity.

I dropped to my knees keeping focused on the depiction of Christ. Tears again filled my bloodshot eyes as I quietly recited a half recollected version of the 'Lord's Prayer'. I then begged of the Lord to spare my son's life. At first the words were difficult to find, but suddenly a verse from an unknown origin filled my head and flowed from my mouth like poetry. I begged of the Lord to allow my son to drink from the cup of life. I prayed that the baby's tainted blood would be made pure and cleansed as men were cleansed by the blood of our Lord.

For the first time in my life, I felt the power of prayer. Even though the doctor's were uncertain about my beautiful baby boy's fate, I felt comforted and confident when I left the chapel a few minutes later.

Two days later, upon my wife's discharge, the family doctor arrived and informed us that our child was in very critical condition and would need an emergency blood transfusion to survive.

Devastated, I made my way back to the little chapel while my wife completed the final discharge paperwork. Exhausted from a lack of sleep over the previous three days, I sat down on a hardwood bench nearest the podium. I focused upon the brilliant cross of gold and said a quiet prayer before drifting into a deep sleep. A few minutes later I found myself standing in a vast field.

The field was vivid, green and alive. It extended beyond the horizon where it sloped into an enormous valley. The day was bright with the sun dancing in the clear blue sky above. The knee high blue-green grass waved back and forth in warm springtime breeze. There was a wonderful serenity about this place. Just as I was getting comfortable with my new surroundings I began to sense something off in the distance. I peered back up into the unblemished sky and visualized a disturbance beyond the horizon. I trembled in fear as I realized a horrible catastrophe was in the midst.

The rapidly approaching tragedy was unlike any I had ever witnessed before. I dropped to my knees when I recognized a great ball of fire approaching from the heavens. I again trembled violently when I realized that the pending ball of fire and doom was not coming to consume me, but that of my infant child.

Somehow my attention was suddenly diverted to a presence from behind. I recovered to my feet to turn and find a man standing several meters to my left. He was old, his pale face was weathered from his many years. Dressed in a top hat and black suit, his apparel was the late nineteenth-early twentieth century american. A thick, hickory wood walking stick supported his short, stalky frame. The ancient soul then removed his focus from the sky above and looked upon me, his young counterpart. As his thick white beard twirled in the strong breeze I recognized a great wisdom about him. The sadness and despair that owned my heart began to subside as I stared upon the classical gentleman. Then for a brief but wonderful moment, I was permitted to read his thoughts. "Believe, and all will be well. Grace has fallen upon your child. For your words were enough." He said without speaking a word. I watched as he turned and walked away, slowly fading into the vastness of this garden called 'Eden'.

The great ball of light exploded in the sky many miles above me and moments later, a shower of flames fell upon the valley floor.

I suddenly awoke to find that I had been sleeping for nearly an hour. I quickly climbed onto the elevator and made my way to the second floor where I found my wife still standing at the admissions/discharge counter. A discouraging look was upon her face as she was conversing with the family doctor. Our doctor, a young attractive woman of thirty-two years, greeted me with a warm yet concerned smile.

"Your are fortunate to have a wife with such great instinct! Had you waited until morning to bring her in, or even two hours later, your son would have been still-born. At least now, with an emergency transfusion, he has a chance. A real good chance!"

The next day the baby received a partial transfusion. The procedure was a success and after thirteen days of ups and downs, Chayce Richard Aites left the hospital fully recovered.

As I pulled the car around to the emergency room entrance to pick up my wife and child, I observed a man standing at the far end of the parking lot. He was focusing upon the massive building known as Cardinal Glennon Childrens Hospital. He was the old man in my dream.

I assisted my wife in securing our newborn son in the car seat. Upon returning to the driver's seat and turning on the ignition, I focused back onto the lot. The old gentleman was gone.

THE BOOK OF RICHARD

CHAPTER SIX

Two weeks after Chayce arrived home from the hospital, I again found myself standing alone upon a vast field. Only this time, I was not sleeping. The field was broken up into quarters by several small, crab apple orchards. Six inches of freshly fallen snow covered the surface.

It was the last day of archery season and I was in pursuit of a Lincoln County whitetail deer. It was a much needed break from the stress I endured from the events that had unfolded over the previous month. It was refreshing to get back to nature.

It was dawn and the yawning sun was just edging up over the horizon as I made my way across the frozen field and into an acre lot of thorn trees and briars. The raspy chatter of black capped chickadees and the barking of an old gray squirrel greeted me as I meandered my way through the thorny vanes. Moments later I stepped out onto a small clearing which I followed before proceeding along the wood's edge.

It was cold, not much above freezing but my visible breath was warm as it was pushed back against my face by the solemn but biting, early morning breeze. A rust colored, red fox, blotted with patches of gray, darted across the trail directly in front of me. A half eaten cottontail rabbit dangled from its mouth.

Fifteen minutes later, I found myself kneeling alongside an old, white oak tree which was to aid in concealing my form. From this vantage point on top a small ridge, I could watch for deer approaching along the valley floor. The ancient creek bed would bend and wind until it ended some one hundred and fifty meters to the west at the edge of a long since harvested corn field.

It was at this spot, in the previous season, that I took my first whitetail buck with a bow.

I was particularly interested in a majestic ten point that I had my eyes on since scouting the area the previous summer. And though I was uncertain, I had not heard any reports of anyone taking the magnificent animal during the early bow or gun seasons.

Scanning the area for any sign of movement, I observed several sets of deer tracks encrusted upon last night's snow. The tracks led down a common trail some twenty meters below my position. The trail extended along the ridge before transversing down over the hill and dispersing into the broken stalks and piles of husks that a few months earlier, was productive field filled of maize.

Within minutes, the tips of my fingers began to numb as the light, loose fitting gloves could not retain the necessary heat needed to aid in circulation. I tried to remain as still as possible but it wasn't long before my body trembled and shivered every time the frigid breeze rode up through the valley engulfing everything within its reach.

Just as I was to recover to my feet and begin walking for warmth, the flicker of a movement caught my eye. When I recognized the movement as one I had grown to know quite well, a surge of adrenaline rushed through my veins, bringing with it, warmth to my frozen limbs. A small herd of whitetails were approaching from the dormant field below.

One of the animals whiffed at the cold, Alberta clipper air. Though the whitetail's sense of smell is extremely keen, I was upwind and the animals were not alerted to my presence.

I remained motionless as the lead deer, a tiny doe, made her way up the trail and stopped fifty meters from my position. She scraped at the frozen ground and snow with her sharp hooves searching for acorns or any vegitation that would provide her with nourishment. She was smaller that I first presumed, maybe seventy pounds. I spent the next several minutes watching her as she leisurely made her way along the winding trail before eventually disappearing out of sight.

Over the next few minutes, two more does climbed the trail before skirting across the small clearing and disappearing into woods on the other side. Discouraged that none of the animals owned antlers, I again began to recover to my feet when another movement caught my attention.

As I peered around the massive hulk of the oak, I observed a much larger animal approaching along the trail. Eventually it stepped into the clearing just twenty meters below me. This deer towered over the previous three and my heart began pounding anxiously as I focused onto the rack that rested upon his handsome head. Resembling two pitchforks standing side by side and on end, all eight bone colored points jetted straight up into the air. Slowly reaching or my bow, I watched as a cloud of vapor jetted several feet before him when he snorted in the mid-January air. Luckily he was looking the other way as I slowly raised the bow, drawing the string and bringing the cold, plastic nock of the arrow to rest against my cheek. I carefully aligned the tip of my red, twenty meter pin with the peep sight. The deer remained motionless as he focused upon something on the far ridge. Though he was not he largest buck I'd ever seen, he was indeed a prize, especially this late in the season when many of the male deer had shed their antlers.

I took a deep breath and rested the sight motionlessly behind his front, left shoulder. The shot was perfect, as a good release would send a razor sharp broadhead into the unsuspecting animal's heart, killing him cleanly and quickly.

THE BOOK OF RICHARD

Suddenly I pulled the bow away from my face and cautiously allowed the string to ride forward without releasing the arrow. This movement caught the animal's attention. He stomped his hoof onto the ground scattering a shower of snow in all directions. A bellow of hot air and vapor extended several feet beyond his flared nostrils as he snorted in protest of my presence. I was a trespasser in his domain. I grunted in response. "You're going to be a father come April or May! Better be ready!" I foolishly hollered into the quiet hills. The buck then turned and high-tailed it for the creek bed below. Within a matter of seconds, he disappeared over the opposite ridge.

I fell back, bottom down onto the cold, padded ground. A satisfied grin came over my numb face. Seasons prior, I would have kicked myself in the ass for allowing such an opportunity to pass me by. The deer was a sure thing I thought. Only twenty meters out and standing broadside, I was no Robin Hood with a compound bow but I practiced a lot before and during the season and was easily capable of placing five out of six arrows, dead center in a Coke can at thirty meters.

For several minutes I would lie in the comfort of the featherly white substance, peering into the layered gray sky above. I thought about the beauty of this place and serenity that surrounded it. There was probably not another human being within three miles. And though I was only a forty-five minute drive from home, at this moment, home was a world away.

The smile began to dissipate when I recalled a harsh reality. The wild places were disappearing, and disappearing fast. Surburbia America was devouring them at an alarming rate, I thought, as the Chesterfield valley and St. Charles County could attest to.

As I sat up and scanned the solemn forest I realized that it might not be here when my son reaches my age. I was lucky enough to have been able to spend much of my leisure time, as an adolescent and adult, fishing and hunting the fresh water trout streams and Alleghany mountains of northwestern PA and the deep rivers and wooded hills and plateaus of eastern-central Missouri.

Tomorrow I would be back to work policing the north St. Louis community in which I patrolled. The serenity and solitude of this place would only be a memory as I would step back into the real world and all of its problems. Drugs, violence, child abuse and too many people would creep back into my life.

I stood to my feet, slinging the bow over my shoulder. As I turned to leave the woods a noise off in the distance got my attention. The buck I had in my sights just minutes prior was focusing upon me from the opposite ridge. He snorted and again stomped his hoof onto the ground apparently, still upset about my trespass. "I'll be back here next season! If you're still here, you'd better beware!" I informed him before leaving.

THE BOOK OF RICHARD

CHAPTER SEVEN

On the following day, while patrolling the eastern end of town, I observed an old, chevy station-wagon approaching my location. I recognized the driver as a resident who had a felony warrant for drug possession and distribution. Being familiar with his record, I was also aware of his prior arrests for robbery and armed criminal action. He was known to carry a small caliber handgun in his waistband.

After completing an immediate U-turn, the driver pulled off onto the shoulder of the roadway, jumped out of the vehicle and fled on foot through several adjoining yards. I quickly exited my patrol car and approached the wagon. Three bags of dope and another bag of cocaine lay on the street below the driver's door. I observed three small children huddled together in the back seat. They were cold because it was a frigid day and the heater in the car didn't work. A woman sat in the front passenger seat. Only thirty years old, she appeared twice her age from years of drug abuse. I told the woman that another officer would be arriving momentarily to see that she and her children got home safely.

I then called for two assist units and proceeded in a foot pursuit of the suspect. I proceeded across three or four yards until I found the suspect's house. The front door was standing wide open. When another officer arrived to assist, we made our way up onto the rigid and weathered porch. As we approached the front door the rancid odor of rotting food or garbage overtook us. "Smells like someone died!" My partner announced as we proceeded into the darkened house. We cautiously entered into a small, empty front room. Th room was almost pitch black as the lightbulbs in the overhead light fixtures were burnt out. Partially illuminating the room with powerful mag lights, the walls were covered in dirt and grease. I observed tiny handprints about three feet above the base board running along the walls exterior. There was an old, musty sofa in the center of the room and a battered 19" television set lying on the floor against the wall.

As I moved the mag light across the room and into the far corner I was startled by a sudden movement. Upon bringing my pistol to eye level I realized that the movement was not human but a cluster of cockroaches meandering along several cracks and crevices. "Damn." I grimaced in disgust.

My partner thought he heard something towards the rear of the house. We quietly entered a small corridor and proceeded into the kitchen where heaps of garbage and spoiled food were piled in a corner. The electric oven was left on with the door open, apparently in an attempt to provide heat for the house. Roaches darted back and forth across the kitchen sink and counter. We then stepped back into the hallway and into a tiny room adjacent to the bathroom. The cold wooden floor was covered in filth and a couple of broken toddler toys lay strewn across its surface. Against a far wall was a bare mattress, torn and soiled.

I then realized that this was where the suspect's children slept and played. A terrible feeling of emptiness and despair made its way from my sternum up into my throat. I became overwhelmed with hopelessness and grief as I reflected upon the three tiny and cold faces in the station-wagon. For one brief, but dangerous moment, sorrow shadowed my alertness and anguish owned my thoughts.

"I'm just tryin' to make a goddamned livin'! The only reason you locked my ass up was because you're a motherf____in' racist!" The suspect shouted as he pounded his fists up against the cold steel bars of the cell door.

It had been nearly an hour since the suspect had been found hiding in the attic but he was still irate about the situation. I explained to him that his habit was destroying those three tiny lives. These children were residing in darkness and filth, hungry and cold because any income provided by government assistance was supporting a drug habit.

"So I'm a drug dealer! I still think you're a racist!" he added before throwing himself down upon the bench and stretching out.

"You have the right to an opinion. I guess that's your point of view." I replied, briefly detered from filling out the arrest form. I then told him that I was aware of racism. I've seen it and am aware that it exists, not only on law enforcement but in every profession the country. Prejudice and bigotry are as old as mankind itself and probably will exist as long as human kind does. Yet the utter despair that I felt for these children and the urgency in which I sought help for them was not typical of a racist. These desperate children were African-Americans.

I explained to him that I saw beyond the color of their skin and into their hearts and soul, and in doing so, I saw into my own. I felt their sorrow and recognized their pain as I peered into a future, which had no sense of love or security. Their world was cold and empty until D.F.S. was brought into the picture. Now maybe they will begin to see the world as all children should, with hope and wonder. Call it racism if you will, but I call it compassion. Points of view don't save lives or remedy society's problems, only love and compassion can do that.

THE BOOK OF RICHARD

As I returned to filling out the booking sheet, I heard snoring coming from the cell. My suspect was fast asleep. "Just call me Ward Cleaver." I mumbled to myself.

CHAPTER EIGHT

Barely sixteen months old, I held him in my arms as we peered out the large, picture-frame window and onto a ruffled robin that was bouncing across the lush, green yard. The child's eyes were beautiful–dark green, maybe hazel–large and curious. His long eye lashes and heavy brow were like framework for a glorious painting. His rounded cheeks and quaint little nose finished the masterpiece.

In those eyes I saw endless possibilities, and in his smile I sensed hope for tomorrow. Here was a tiny human being, not yet molded by his parents or scathed by society.

Free of iniquity and incapable of sin, he questioned not why or how, but loved his parents unconditionally. In my arms I held the answer to all mankind's problems. In my heart I was understanding the Lord's unconditional love.

As the world was confined for the moment, we were on the inside looking out. Then the bird suddenly took to the wing and ended up in a yard beyond his view. A look of confusion came over his tiny face. Then grief. "Birdie go." He quietly gestured as he pointed towards the horizon. My heart became a bit saddened when I sensed his despair. Something as simple as a scavenging robin, searching for earthworms and insects, and the pleasure that accompanied it, was lost for the moment. Disappointment overcame joy as a ball of tears swelled upon his eyes. When I kissed him on the forehead as a sign of reassurement, the wonderful smile returned.

As he peered into my eyes and I into his, and incredible sensation came over me. A wonderful feeling of joy and well being rushed into my nostrils before encircling my soul. For I was looking into the eyes of God and back beyond this present time. I was observing the true creation. Spiritually flawless and incapable of sin, this was in his image that man was originally created.

Yet as fast as I had been absorbed in this joyous feeling, my soul suddenly succumbed to grief and complete despair. The television was showing an old news segment on the war in Rawanda. I turned and watched as the bodies of children floated down a river overflowing in blood. Their lifeless bodies too numerous to count. Another segment showed hundreds of tiny children being dumped into mass, unmarked graves. They were the victims of war created by men.

How could we permit such atrocities? Why couldn't we see how truly precious our children are? Is there a future for them?

CHAPTER NINE

A journey in the following week led me back to the place of my youth. It is a place that I speak of often. It was also vacation and time to visit the in-laws and the last remnants of my clan.

One day during the week-long stay, I found some time to myself. Therefore I made my way across the tiny town and climbed a quiet hill named 'Piscah'. Several minutes later I stepped into the woods. As I walked through the wooded hills I found that nothing had changed. The forest was thick, green and full of life. The smell and warmth of spring filled the air. The old path that I walked was as clear now as it was then and my sacred places remain unharmed.

I followed the path–once a fire road–approximately two miles up onto the highest peak and to a place called 'Big Rocks'. Remnants of the ice age deposited by massive glaciers as they cut out the Alleghany valley, some of the boulders were as big as a two-story house.

I worked my way to the point of the peak until I came to mass known as 'Eagle Rock'. The rock contained a base stone as wide as a baseball diamond and reached to fifteen feet in height. On top of it rested another boulder as big as a bus, extending another ten feet in the air.

The angles of the rocks made for easy climbing and it wasn't long before I was standing on top the monolith. From here I could see over most of the heavy, May foliage and down onto the village of Rouseville which sat along the oil creek valley.

I spent countless afternoons upon this rock as a boy. The serenity of it all was wonderful as there was no place like it in

THE BOOK OF RICHARD

my world. I sat down upon the rock and focused into the clear, blue sky above. I then did something that was a common practice here, in my youth, I prayed. I gave thanks for my son and the miracle that took place when his condition was grave. I then gave thanks for all the good things in my life and I asked for forgiveness for my iniquity. As the prayer came to an end a sudden sadness overcame me. I was in doubt–In doubt of my son's and his generation's future. I felt that I was being a fool to doubt, especially after all that had happened over the previous year, but I couldn't help it.

God had given us the ten commandments to live by and yet we tossed them aside a long time ago. Our liberal society was making a mockery of morality and family values and the end result was just beginning. Had we stuck by those commandments there would have been no need for a constitution or man's law.

As I made my way down the face of the rock I suddenly remembered that it was here that I had hidden the most important document of my life. It was the recording of a vision I had as a teenager which changed my life forever. Written down on a heavy piece of parchment that was given to me by my grandfather at that time. The piece was a remnant from the early twentieth century. It was almost as thick as cardboard and as sturdy. I rolled the document up in scroll form and secured it with a piece of leather string taken from a moccasin. The scroll was then placed inside a mason jar that was large enough to hold two quarts of whole, stewed tomatoes.

I somewhat recalled where I had placed the jar, therefore I made my way to the rear of the mass until I came upon a shelf created between the two rocks. I thrust myself up onto the edge of the shelf and cautiously crawled though the narrow opening of the sleeve. The sleeve resembled a tiny cave and was about four feet in height and twelve feet deep. It was just light enough inside that I didn't need a flashlight, yet still dark enough that I didn't want to reach into a crevice and be greeted by an eastern diamondback.

After spending ten minutes in the cave searching for the scroll, I gave up discouraged. I figured that somebody had found it, or it became a victim of the elements. Maybe I just wasn't looking in the right place.

As I pushed my way back out of the sleeve I lost my grasp and fell some fifteen feet to the ground below. As I landed on my backside I heard a loud crunch. "Shit! I must have busted my ass!" I shouted in disgust. Yet I felt fine as I recovered to my feet. Wiping leaves and dirt from the rear of my jeans I observed a thick sliver of broken glass sticking up from under the topsoil. I kneeled down and began brushing decaying leaves and two inches of topsoil aside. There lying in the dirt was several large fragments of the mason jar. As I tossed the slivers of glass aside I found my scroll, still intact and still secured by the dry rotted piece of leather.

"I found you." I said to myself as I held the scroll in the air above my head. Not remembering most of the contents I unraveled the leather string and let it drop upon the forest floor. I then unrolled the scroll and was dismayed to find that the words, written in black ink, were mottled and blotted. Unreadable, apparently moisture had gotten into the jar and contaminated the treasured piece.

Before tossing the illegible testimony onto the ground, I looked it over one last time. I scanned the scroll from line to line until I came to a hidden fold at the bottom of the document. When I unfolded it at the crease I was startled to find a line in perfect order. The ink appeared as fresh and legible, as it was when written more than sixteen years earlier.

THE BOOK OF RICHARD

It read 'Lest I forget, I shall never doubt again. For I have seen the Lord Jesus, and he lives…'

"For God so loved the world, that he gave his only begotten Son, that whosoever believeth in him should not perish, but have everlasting life." (John 3:16)

CHILDREN OF THE WORLD

Little child,
You needn't cry anymore,
He's here to save you,
Save you from war,
He's seen the anguish,
He knows of your pain,
And the evil will leave here,
For this is why he came,
So run in joy,
And not in fear,
Sing songs of happiness,
Wipe away the tears,
Tell the children to look to the sky,
And heaven they can see,
For he loves the children dearly,
And they love him...
     Richard W. Aites (1990)

THE BOOK OF RICHARD

T.B.O.R

*'FOR I SHALL WRITE IT DOWN AND TELL IT, SO THE WORLD SHALL KNOW
AND THAT I MAY NEVER FORGET.'*

THE CHILD WAS NOT YET A DAY OLD WHEN DEATH ARRIVED TO GREET HIM. AN UNWELCOME VISITOR, IT STOLE THE BREATH FROM HIS VERY LUNGS AND MADE HIS BLOOD BITTER. AS DEATH SAT BESIDE HIM AND CLUTCHED HIS TINY HAND, A GREAT DARKNESS OVERCAME ME. I SOUGHT COMFORT FROM THOSE AROUND ME, YET I FOUND NONE. A MULTITUDE OF QUESTIONS WERE WITHOUT ANSWERS AS THE DOCTORS WERE PUZZLED AND THE NURSES CONFUSED. I WATCHED AS DEATH BEGAN TO LEAD MY CHILD DOWN THAT PERILOUS PATH.

THEN I WAS DRAWN TO A HOLY PLACE WHERE I KNEELED BELOW A CROSS OF GOLD. I FOUND COMFORT IN PRAYER AS I BEGGED OF THE LORD TO ALLOW MY INFANT SON TO DRINK FROM TH CUP OF LIFE. I PRAYED FOR HIS TAINTED BLOOD TO BE MADE PURE AND CLEANSED, AS WE WERE CLEANSED OF OUR SIN BY THE BLOOD OF THE LORD.

AS I PRAYED BOTH DAY AND NIGHT, I SOON WITNESSED DEATH BEGIN TO RELEASE ITS

RELENTLESS HOLD. I OBSERVED THE LIFE SLOWLY RETURN BACK INTO MY BEAUTIFUL CHILD'S BODY. BEFORE LONG, DEATH HAD DEPARTED AND NOW MY SON WAS WITHIN THE ARMS OF THE LORD, AND THE LORD RETURNED HIM TO ME.

    I HAVE ALWAYS BELIEVED IN THE HEALING POWER OF OUR LORD AND SAVIOR, YET I QUESTIONED HIS WILL AND WAS A FOOL TO DOUBT HIM. ONCE AGAIN, THE LORD HATH REMOVED ME FROM THE DARKNESS AND BROUGHT ME FORTH INTO THE LIGHT. I WAS WITHOUT HOPE AND YET HE ANSWERED MY PRAYERS.

    SO BEWARE, FOR THOUGH MANY SEE THE COMING OF THE NEW MILLENNIUM AS A TIME OF TURMOIL AND REVELATION. KNOW YE THAT THIS IS TRULY A TIME OF MIRACLES. FOR I AM NO LONGER BLIND TO THE VAST PINNACLES OF LIGHT AMONGST THE WHOLE OF DARKNESS. IT IS A FOOL WHO WATCHES FOR A MOUNTAIN TO MOVE OR THE WATERS OF A SEA TO PART AND NOT RECOGNIZE THAT HIS ALMIGHTY HAND IS AT WORK EVERY DAY WITHIN OUR VERY LIVES....

                                    RICHARD W. AITES